Int. Order of Good Templars

Ritual of the Independent Order of Good Templars

for Subordinate Lodges

Int. Order of Good Templars

Ritual of the Independent Order of Good Templars
for Subordinate Lodges

ISBN/EAN: 9783337334154

Printed in Europe, USA, Canada, Australia, Japan

Cover: Foto ©Andreas Hilbeck / pixelio.de

More available books at **www.hansebooks.com**

RITUAL

INDEPENDENT ORDER

OF

GOOD TEMPLARS,

FOR

SUBORDINATE LODGES,

UNDER THE JURISDICTION OF THE

RIGHT WORTHÝ GRAND LODGE OF NORTH AMERICA.

ADOPTED AT CLEVELAND SESSION,
MAY 24, 1864.

CHICAGO:
PUBLISHED BY THE RIGHT WORTHY GRAND LODGE.
1864.

DIAGRAM OF GOOD TEMPLARS' HALL.

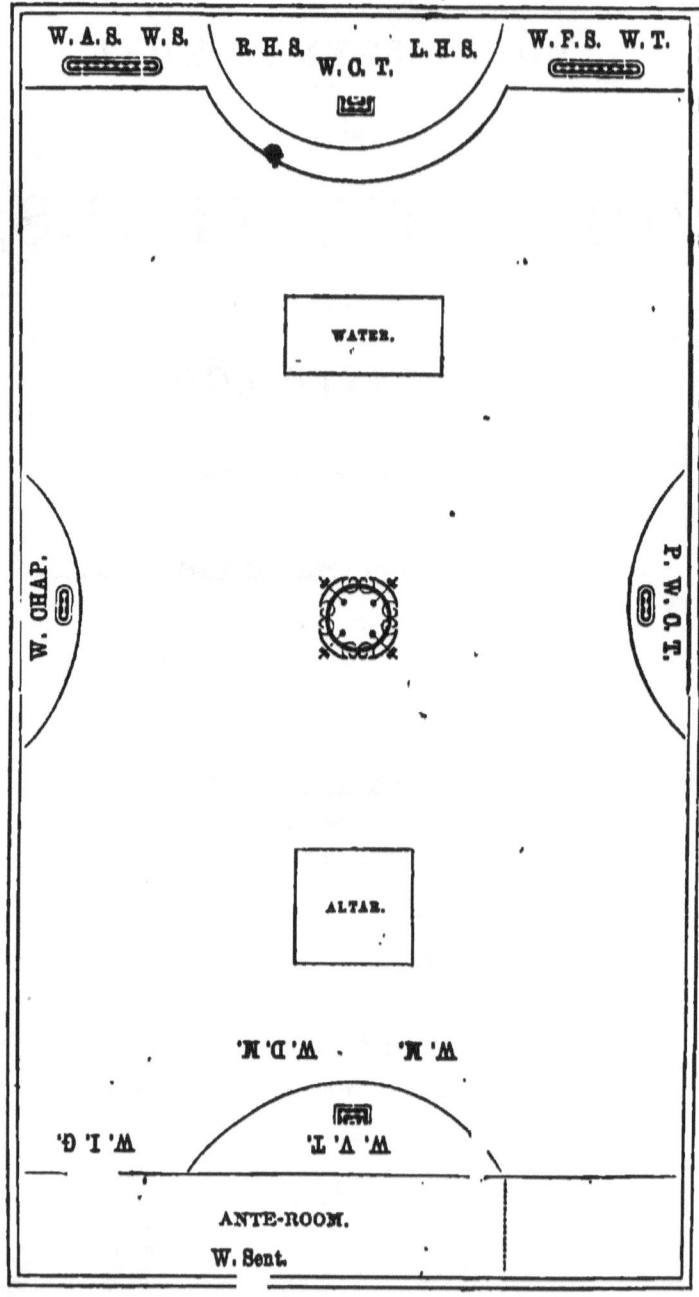

ORDER OF BUSINESS.

1.—Opening Ceremonies.
2.—Roll of Officers and Appointments *pro-tem.*
3.—Reading Journal, and action thereon.
4.—Reports of Investigating Committees.
5.—Balloting on Candidates.
6.—Initiatory Ceremonies.

INTERMISSION.

7.—Propositions for Membership, and reference
  to Committees.
8.—Reports; Special Committees; Sickness;
  Violations.
9.—Charges preferred and referred to Committees.
10.—Reports of Officers; Trustees; Finance
  Committee.
11.—Application for Degrees.
12.—Election; Installation, and other Special
  Orders.
13.—Unfinished Business.
14.—Communications, and New Business.
15.—Good of the Order; Lectures, Essays,
  Speeches, Papers, etc.
16.—Closing Ceremonies.

GENERAL RULES.

1. Whenever an obligation is to be administered, the Lodge should always be called to their feet.

2. The attitude to be assumed on receiving the obligation, is, the right hand upon the heart. The open Bible should lie upon the altar, in front of the candidate.

3. Should candidates refuse to assent to the Obligation, the Initiation cannot proceed, but the W. M. will conduct such candidates to the ante-room.

4. Officers entering the Lodge room and reporting to the W. C. T., give the salutation to that Officer as they report.

5. When the Lodge is visited by the Officers of the Grand Lodge, or their Representatives, officially, it should rise as they enter the room and give the salutation.

RITUAL.

OPENING.

[*When the hour arrives for opening the Lodge, the W. C. T. (and in his absence the W. V. T., or a P. W. C. T.) will take the chair and call the Lodge to order.*]

W. C. T. We are now about to open the Lodge. All not members of the Order will please retire. The Officers and Members will clothe themselves in appropriate regalia and assume their respective positions.

The Worthy Vice Templar will see that the Guards of the Lodge are at their proper places,

---

* These Explanatory Notes and Special Rules, in *italic*, are for the information and guide of the Officers only, and are not to be spoken in any instance during the Ceremony.

and that they are correct in the Quarterly Password, Explanation and Signals.

[*The W. C. T. will now make such pro-tem. appointments as are necessary to open the Lodge.*]

The Marshal and Deputy will communicate to me the Pass-word and Explanation of the present term, after which they will ascertain and report if all present are in possession of the same.

[*The W. M. commences with the L. H. S.; the .W. D. M. with the R. H. S. reporting each failure to give them correctly as it occurs. Should there be any present not in possession of the Quarterly Pass-word and Explanation, and not entitled to the same, the W. C. T. should require them to leave the room; if entitled, the W. C. T. will communicate them at once. On completing examination, the Marshal and Deputy resume their respective positions, and report all correct.*]

●   ●

[*Officers that respond rise.*]

W. C. T. Worthy Officers: what are your respective duties?

W. V. T. To assist you in preserving order;

allow none to enter or retire during the Opening, Closing, or Initiatory Ceremonies, unless directed by you; to have charge of the anteroom of this Lodge, and in conjunction with the Guards, enforce the rules of the Order in relation to the same.

P. W. C. T. To receive and recognize the salutation, and see that Members are properly clothed in regalia.

W. S. To keep a correct record of the proceedings of this meeting.

W. F. S. To keep just and true accounts between this Lodge and myself; between the Lodge and its members, and pay all money received to the Worthy Treasurer.

W. T. To safely keep all money of the Lodge, and pay the same only on the order of the Worthy Chief Templar and Worthy Secretary.

W. M. To see that all present are qualified to remain; to keep the regalia in order; introduce candidates, and attend to visiting members.

W. Chap. It is my duty and privilege to
conduct the devotional exercises of the Lodge
Let us look to God for his blessing.

[*or, "Let us listen to the teachings of Divine Inspira-
tion" (in case a passage of Scripture is read). An
extempore prayer can be used if preferred.*]

●   ●   ●

PRAYER.

Our Father, who art in Heaven, we thank
Thee, that Thy protecting care has been over
us, and ours, during another week; and that
we are permitted again to meet together around
our common altar, under circumstances of so
great mercy. Do Thou be pleased to pardon
all our transgressions, and forgive us for having
loved and served Thee so feebly. As we are
met to promote the great interests of the Temperance cause, may we be enlightened and
strengthened, so as to make our plans and acts
most potent for good. We would commend to
Thee the suffering everywhere, and especially
the inebriate and his family; and wilt Thou
help us to work for the good of those thus
unfortunate. Bless, O Lord, the organization

to which we belong, and all Temperance effort in whatever direction, and in Thine own good time, may everything that can intoxicate be driven from our midst, and the clouds that have so long darkened our sky, be scattered by the golden beams of truth and Temperance. Do Thou guide us in our deliberations this evening, through the journey of life ever lead us, and finally bring us to Thyself in Thine own Kingdom, which we ask in the name of Thy dear Son, our Redeemer. *Amen.*

W. C. T. Officers and Members: our respective duties are plain, and I need not urge their faithful discharge upon all. A nobler moral object than ours never called true men and women together in council. We are here to work. Let us do it, and so advance our common cause, and honor God. Please sing our Opening Ode.

[*The W. C. T. will announce which Ode will be sung.*]

OPENING ODES.

1. Air—" *Watchman.*"

Friends of Temperance, welcome here,
　Cheerful are our hearts to-day;
Tell us—we would gladly hear—
　How our cause speeds on its way.

Here we pledge ourselves anew,
　Not to touch the drunkard's drink;
Proving faithful, proving true,
　We will from no duty shrink.

2. Air—" *The Battle Cry of Freedom.*"

We are gathering for the conflict, with earnest hearts and true,
　Shouting the battle cry of Temperance;
The world will bless our progress in the work we have to do;
　Shouting the battle cry of Temperance.
Cold water forever, hurrah! then, hurrah!
Down with the wine glass—up with our star;
As we gather for a right cause, with earnest hearts and true,
　Shouting the battle cry of Temperance.

W. C. T. I now declare the Lodge open for the transaction of business.

●

[*The W. C. T should require all the members in the ante-room to enter, and then proceed with the usual Order of Business.*]

INITIATION.

[*When the Lodge is ready for Initiation, the W. C. T. will direct the W. M. to retire to the ante-room, and ascertain if there are candidates in waiting; and the W. M., in reporting candidates, should announce their names in full in open Lodge, that the W. C. T. and W. S. may satisfy themselves that the persons have been duly elected.*]

W. C. T. The Past Worthy Chief Templar and Financial Secretary will repair to the ante-room, propound the usual questions, and collect the fees and dues.

[*The P. W. C. T. and W. F. S. will retire; the following questions are to be answered in the affirmative:*]

P. W. C. T. Will you be obedient to all the laws and rules of this Institution, they not conflicting with your duties as a citizen or a Christian?

Answer. I will.

P. W. C. T. Will you take a solemn pledge to abstain forever from the use of, or giving to others as a beverage, anything that will intoxicate?

Answer. I will.

P. W. C. T. Do you believe in the existence of Almighty God, the Ruler and Governor
of all things ?

Answer. I do.

[*These questions having been answered in the affirmative, and the fee collected, the Officers return to the Lodge-
room, salute the W. C. T., and report.*]

W. F. S. Worthy Chief Templar, the fee is
paid.

P. W. C. T. Worthy Chief Templar, the
questions are properly answered.

W. C. T. The Marshal and Deputy will
now repair to the ante-room, and introduce the
candidate.

[*If but one candidate, only one officer need retire.
The W. M. conducting the candidate to the door, gives
three distinct raps.*]

I. G. Worthy Vice Templar, there is an
alarm at the inner gate.

W. V. T. You will attend to it.

I. G.   It is our Marshal, accompanied by a *friend*, who *seeks* admission to our Lodge.

W. V. T.   Admit them.

●   ●   ●

[*While singing, the W. M. conducts the candidates slowly around the room, stopping at the close of the Ode in front of the chair of the W. C. T.*]

1. Air—"*Savior, like a shepherd lead us.*"

Welcome, welcome to our Order,
  We shall need your help and care;
In the harvest fields of Temperance,
  You shall have a rightful share.
Welcome, welcome,
  Heaven bless you! is our prayer;
Welcome, welcome,
  Heaven bless you! is our prayer.

2. Air—*Harwell.*

Welcome, stranger, to this Temple,
  To our altar now advance;
Join our band of valiant soldiers,
  Strike for Right and Temperance.
Hearts united cheer you on,
Honor, pleasure will be won,
Welcome, stranger, to this Temple,
Welcome, welcome, welcome here!

●

W. M. Worthy Chief Templar, allow me to introduce to you our *friend,* who, after due trial, *wishes* to become *a member* of our Order.

W. C. T. My *friend,* we give you a cordial welcome.

R. H. S. Welcome! Here you will find encouragement in every laudable purpose.

L. H. S. Welcome! Here you will find friends in the hour of peril.

W. C. T. It rejoices our hearts that henceforth your services are to be given to the great Temperance reform, and that to this end, you desire to unite your influence with ours. This place is sacredly dedicated to the cause of Temperance, and you see here the entire family circle around one common altar, fully determined to reclaim the fallen, and save others from falling. The enemy with which we have to contend is crafty and powerful, and to resist such a foe successfully will require our mightiest efforts. All have felt his power, or suffered more or less from his destructive influences. In every walk of life, intemperance, like an undying worm, has gnawed at the vitals and corrupted the life-blood of the fairest, ablest and purest of earth. We aim to unite all moral and social elements of society in an unceasing warfare upon this giant evil. Our hearts and hands are ever open, to lift up those who are sunk low in the scale of human degradation, and restore them to family, friends, and society, as well as to save the young, pure and virtuous from ever falling into the snares of the tempter.

You will now be required to take upon *yourself* a solemn obligation of total abstinence, and to bind *yourself* to our laws; but, as you have already been assured, there is nothing in this obligation inconsistent with your duties arising from any of the relations of life. It is an obligation earnest in its nature, imperative in its requirements, and lifelong in its duration. Regarding it thus, are you still willing to proceed?

Candidate. I am.

Worthy Marshal, you will now present our *friend* to the Worthy Vice Templar for obligation.

[The W. M. and candidate will remain standing at the Altar while one of the following Odes is sung :]

1. AIR—*America.*

God of the Temperance cause,
Bless Those who seek thy laws,
   Owning their power;
Be Thou to them a shield,
Teach them thy sword to wield
Upon temptation's field,
   In sin's dark hour.

2. AIR—*Pleyel's Hymn.*

God of Mercy! be Thou near,
While these vows are spoken here;
Shield the victor, guard and guide
Where the lurking tempters hide;
Man may strive, but Thou alone
Must the final conquest crown.

W. M. Worthy Vice Templar, by direction of our Worthy Chief Templar, I here present our *friend* for Obligation.

W. V. T. You will place your right *hand* upon your *heart* and assent to the following

OBLIGATION.

You, in a full belief in the existence and power of Almighty God, and in the presence of these witnesses, do solemnly and unreservedly promise that you will not make, buy, sell, use, furnish, or cause to be furnished to others, as a beverage, any spirituous or malt liquors, wine or cider; and that, in all honorable ways, you will discountenance their use in the community. You also promise, that you will not reveal any of the private work or business of this Order to any one not entitled to know the same, and that in all things you will yield a cheerful obedience to all our laws, rules and usages. You also promise, that you will not knowingly wrong a member of this Order, or see one wronged, and that you will do all in your power to promote the good of this Order and to advance the cause of Temperance.

Do you thus promise?

Candidate. I do.

W. M. (and all the Lodge in concert.) We are witnesses of your solemn obligation.

W. C. T. The Chaplain will now invoke the Divine blessing.

PRAYER.

W. Chap. Our Father who art in Heaven, we now implore thy blessing upon *this friend,* who has just assumed a high and responsible obligation, and whose influence is henceforth to be united with ours to drive Intemperance from the land. Give *him* strength to discharge every duty arising from this new relation, and grace to redeem every pledge. May *he* have strength to resist every temptation; and, in Thy hands, become an honored instrument in leading many to virtue and peace. Be pleased to graciously bless us, in this addition to our numbers and influence; and may our union prove a blessing to us and many others, and an honor to Thy great name; to whom be glory and dominion for ever and ever. *Amen.*

[*The Candidate will turn and face the W. C. T. The Officers remain standing.*]

P. W. C. T. This vow we have all taken and kept. Let the fidelity with which it is kept by you, be your glory and your shield. Remember your vow.

W. C. T. None but the brave dare take such a vow; but a true heart and determined purpose will accomplish much. Remember your vow.

W. Chap. A Templar's vow is registered in heaven; as you value your standing here and your peace in eternity, keep that vow sacred to the end of life. Remember your obligation.

W. V. T. Your sacred honor is given to us that you will keep your obligation. He that is faithful in little, will be faithful in much. Your character is at stake in your vow. Keep it, then, to the end of life.

Marshal, you will continue to act as guide to our *friend.*

[The W. M. conducts them around the room while singing.]

1. Am—*"Beautiful Star."*

Hail! all hail! O friends of Right!
Keep the vows you've made to-night!
Let no purple wine be poured
As you gather at the board.
    Destroying wine,
    Destroying wine,
Wine, wine of the drunkard,
Taste not, O taste not the wine!

2. Am—*Auld Lang Syne.*

Come, friends and brethren, all unite,
    In songs of hearty cheer;
Our cause speeds onward in its might—
    Away with doubt and fear.
We give the pledge, we join the hand,
    Resolved on victory;
We are a bold, determined band,
    And strike for liberty.

The cup of death no more we take;
    That cup no more we give;
It makes the head, the bosom, ache—
    Ah! who can drink and live?
We give the pledge, we join the hand,
    Resolved on victory;
We are a bold, determined band,
    And strike for liberty.

[The W. M. will lead the Candidate just in front of the Altar, facing the W. C. T., and the officers rise as they respond.]

W. C. T. Wine is a mocker, strong drink is raging; and whosoever is deceived thereby is not wise. He that loveth pleasure shall be poor: he that loveth wine shall not be rich.

P. W. C. T. Be not among wine-bibbers; for the drunkard shall come to poverty, and drowsiness shall clothe a man with rags.

W. C. T. How exceedingly strong is wine; it causeth all men to err that drink it: Let no drunkenness go with thee in thy journey, for it diminisheth strength; it maketh wounds!

W. Chap. Woe unto him that giveth his neighbor drink, that putteth the bottle to him and maketh him drunken also!

W. V. T. He that contemneth small things shall fall by little and little. Show not thy valiantness in wine, for strong drink hath destroyed many.

W. C. T. Who hath sorrow? Who hath woe? Who hath babbling? Who hath contentions? Who hath wounds without cause? Who hath redness of eyes?

W. M. They that tarry long at the wine; they that go to seek mixed wine.

W. C. T. Then look not thou upon the wine when it is red, when it giveth its color in the cup, when it moveth itself aright. At the last it biteth like a serpent, and stingeth like an adder!

Worthy Marshal, you will now conduct *this friend* to our Worthy Chaplain.

W. M. Worthy Chaplain, our *friend awaits* further instruction.

W. Chap. My *friend*, the gems of truth which we have just given you, are from Divine revelation; treasure them in your *heart*, and it will be well with you now and hereafter. Study well the volume from which they are taken, for therein are found words of eternal life. The Scriptures teach Temperance in all things, and declare that no drunkard shall inherit the Kingdom of Heaven. In your hours of study, consult them; in your hours of reverie, meditate upon their teachings; and in the hour of temptation, look to that Word which was in the beginning, is now, and shall be evermore, for strength; and at the feet of the Son of God, learn the lesson of faith, hope, and charity; for if you love them that love you, and do good to those who bestow their favors upon you, what do ye more than others? I charge you to love God, and keep his commandments; let your hope be ardent, your faith strong, and your charity like the bounty of God, who sendeth the rain and the sunshine alike upon the just and upon the unjust.

Worthy Marshal, you will conduct *this friend* to the Worthy Vice Templar, who will give *him* further instructions.

W. M. Worthy Vice Templar, *this friend* is on *his* way to learn more of the teachings of our Order.

W. V. T. I welcome you on your way. Many have gone the same road before you, and we hope many may come after. You have listened to the voice of revelation, but Temperance is not alone taught in the Scriptures. In nature we find no strong drinks—nothing that can intoxicate. The Almighty and All-wise prepared but one drink—pure water.

This He furnished bountifully, and sent it coursing through the earth, rushing down the hill-side, glancing in the sunbeams, bounding through the valley, distilling in the dew, and treasured in the mighty deep. Animated nature needs no other drink. Man alone, whom God made upright, is dissatisfied, and has sought out many inventions. Placed at the head of all animate creation, man is the only creature that sinks below his element—below the brute —by yielding to his strange and acquired appetite. Think well of these things, and I charge you to be satisfied with the drink furnished by One wiser than we.

Marshal, conduct our *friend* to the Past Worthy Chief Templar, who will still further advance *him* on *his* way.

W. M. Past Worthy Chief Templar, I am directed to present *this friend* to you for further instruction.

P. W. C. T. My *friend*, it gives me pleasure to assist you in advancing. You have heard the warnings of Scripture; you have listened to the teachings of nature; but lessons of Temper-

anco are not confined to these. History lifts
its warning voice, saying,—BEWARE OF STRONG
DRINK! It tells of heroes, prophets, priests and·
kings, fallen by its potent power. It shows
that neither power, genius, learning, position or
strength are proof against it. Our own obser-
vation confirms this testimony. We have seen
the tears of the widow and orphan; heard the
low, sad wail of agony sent up by broken
hearts. We have seen bright hopes and pros-
pects blasted; the innocence of youth grown
old with the deformity of ignorance and want;
beauty clothed with rags and shame, and man-
hood shorn of its glory, each repeating daily
the sad warning of the past—BEWARE OF THESE
DRINKS! For protection against their deadly
and seductive influences, and to hasten the hour
when the means of intoxication shall be driven
from our land, are we banded together here.
(*Stepping down and taking the candidate by the
hand*,) I now welcome you to our Lodge—our
fraternal home. Abide with us. Here you
are safe. Remain with us, for the destroyer
can never enter here. Ever have before you
the Divine rule, as though it were written in
letters of living light, "Whatsoever ye would

that others should do unto you, do ye even so unto them." Thus, you will live to a good and noble purpose: the memories of the past will be pleasant, and our future glorious.

You will now accompany our Marshal to the desk of the Financial Secretary, and sign the Constitution; then to the Worthy Chief Templar for the closing ceremonies.

1. Air—*America.*

Long live our temple bright,
Offspring of truth and light,
 Sent from above!
Long may our Brothers stand,
And Sisters—glorious band—
Strong pillars in our land,
 Our pride and love!

2. Air—*Old Hundred.*

Now bound by honor's sacred laws,
Be faithful to our holy cause;
Let truth preserve each member's fame,
Nor curses blast our honored name.

Then welcome to our Unionhood,
A cheerful welcome to the good;
Long live our Order's great renown,
And happiness each member crown!

Stand firm in truth while life shall last,
․ Nor let the blight fall on thy way;
Our hopes, may treason never blast;
 Our trust, no Judas e'er betray.

3. Am—"*Lift your heads, the day is breaking.*"

To our noble cause forever,
  Be a steady beacon light;
Let no deed or word e'er sever
  Those who gather here to-night.
Firm in principles of Temperance,
  Turn the wine-king from his throne,
Keeping always in remembrance,
  God, Great God, is King alone.

W. M. Worthy Chief Templar, our *friend has* traveled the circuit of our Lodge, and now *comes* to you for the closing instructions and ceremonies.

W. C. T. You have now undertaken a life-long work, and we expect that henceforth your labors and influence will be with us and for us; that you will be present at all of our meetings, and that our association here and elsewhere will be mutually pleasant and profitable. I charge you to consider well the lessons of this Lodge. Of necessity they have been brief: ponder them in your mind, and as you advance in our noble Order, they will be more fully exemplified and set forth.

We have signs of recognition, test and pass-words, grips and signals, which I will now give.

[*The W. C. T. will here give the instructions.*]

The members will now form our circle of unity.

●   ●   ●

[*The members form a circle, joining hands around the candidate and officers; the W. C. T., R. H. S., and L. H. S., on one side of the fountain, or table on which are the glasses of water, the W. M. and D. M. with the candidate on the opposite side, and in front of the officers named.*]

W. C. T. By the authority of the Grand Lodge of the Independent Order of Good Templars, I proclaim *this person a member* of this Lodge; and *he is* hereby declared to be entitled to all the rights, privileges and protection guaranteed to members by our Constitution, By-Laws, Rules and usages.

[*The R. H. S. and L. H. S. hand the W. C. T., W. M., D. M. and candidate glasses of water.*]

And in this pure element of water, God's only beverage, we mutually pledge a life-long fidelity to our sacred cause. (*Officers and candidate drink.*)

1. AIR—" *There's much good cheer.*"—(*Cracovienne.*)

Fill all your sparkling glasses high,
With health that wine can never buy;
Cold water, full of strength and life,
Will nerve our weakest for the strife;
Flash out a draught of water cold,
With cheerful faces, young and old,
'Twas given a blessing from the sky,
Then fill your sparkling glasses high!

2. AIR—"*Sparkling and Bright.*"

Sparkling and bright, in its liquid light,
Is the water in our glasses;
'Twill give you health, 'twill give you wealth,
Ye lads and rosy lasses!
O! then resign your ruby wine,
Each smiling son and daughter;
There's nothing so good for the youthful blood,
Or sweet as the sparkling water!

W. C. T. Thus are you surrounded by friends upon whom you have fraternal claims; this circle which you see around us being the emblem of perpetual friendship. The union of hands signifies the union of hearts, and purpose and effort in our great work. Before you join hands with us, we will invest you, as all worthy members should be, with proper regalia. (*The R. H. S. or L. H. S., or both, officiate.*) It is hoped you will ever wear *this badge* with pleasure and profit to *yourself,* and honor to this institution and the cause of Temperance.

You will now take your place, and form a part of our circle.

[*The W. C. T. and Supporters resume their respective stations.*]

Now, as we all stand united around our common altar, having plighted our faith together beneath our sacred standard, behold how good and how pleasant it is for brethren to dwell together in unity. May the pleasant ties that now bind us together be severed only in death.

Air—*Zion.*

Hail we now our new made member,
   Linked with us in friendship's chain;
Kind and faithful to each other,
   Love will soothe our woes and pain;
     Thus progressing,
   Blessings follow in our train.

[*During the recess for congratulations, the candidate should be made acquainted with all present.*]

CLOSING.

W. C. T. Worthy Financial Secretary, what are the receipts of the evening?

W. F. S. The receipts are * * * Worthy Chief Templar.

W. C. T. Has the Treasurer received the same?

W. T. I have, Worthy Chief Templar.

❂ ❂ ❂

W. C. T. Worthy officers and members, we are about to close this meeting. I thank you for your presence and attention this evening: let us now listen to our parting counsel.

W. V. T. Brothers and Sisters, let us not forget the principles enjoined upon us by our Order. At our altar we have given our most sacred promises to abstain from all that can intoxicate, and by all just means in our power to banish intemperance. We desire the presence of all, and shall expect you here at our next meeting.

W. C. T. We must now separate, to mingle again in the pursuits and temptations of life. In your respective callings, shun the way of evil doers, and exhibit by your integrity that the labors and teachings of our Lodge are not in vain.

We will now sing our closing ode.

CLOSING ODES.

1. Air—*Sicilian Hymn.* •

Heavenly Father! give thy blessing,
 While we now this meeting end;
On our mind each truth impressing,
 That may to thy glory tend.
Save from all intoxication,
 From its fountain may we flee;
When assailed by strong temptation,
 Put our trust alone in thee.

2. Air—*Cheney.*

Great God! hear thou our prayer to-night,
 The foes of Temperance may we brave;
Guide all our faltering steps aright,
 Our fellow men from ruin save.

3. Air—*Ward.*

May friendship's chain be ever bright,
 And charity and love increase;
May Providence protect the right,
 Reclaim the wrong, establish peace.

W. C. T. You will now give attention to the Closing service by the Worthy Chaplain.

[*The Chaplain will pronounce a benediction, offer a short extempore prayer, or use the following :*]

PRAYER.

Our Father who art in Heaven, we thank Thee for the privilege of the present meeting, and for whatever good we may have been enabled to accomplish. Pardon, we entreat Thee, whatever in our present intercourse may have been displeasing to Thee, in thought, word or deed. Deepen every conviction of duty; and strengthen every earnest resolution of amendment. Accompany us to our several homes, and keep us and all our loved ones there ever under the shadow of Thy wing. Guide us by Thy counsels while we live, and finally receive us into that temple not made with hands, eternal in the heavens. For thine is the kingdom, and power, and the glory forever. · *Amen.*

W. C. T. The meeting is now closed.

INSTALLATION.

[*The proper installing Officer is the G. W. C. T., (or, in his absence, a D. G. W. C. T.)   When the Lodge is ready for installation, the G. W. C. T. will quietly appoint a G. W. S. and a G. W. M., and retire to the ante-room.*]

W. C. T. Worthy Marshal, our Lodge is duly prepared for the installation of its officers, and the Grand Worthy Chief Templar is in waiting in our ante-room to install them.   You will now retire and introduce him, with such representatives of the officers of the Grand Lodge as may accompany him.

[*W. M. retires and introduces the officers.*]

W. M. Worthy Chief Templar, I have the honor and pleasure of presenting to you the Grand Worthy Chief Templar, who is here for the purpose of installing the officers of this Lodge.   He also brings with him *these Brothers*

(*and Sisters*), whom he has selected to repre-
sent the Grand Lodge.

[*All give the salutation except in public installations.*]

W. C. T. It is with pleasure that I welcome
you within our Lodge. Our officers are elected,
and waiting to be installed. It will be our
pleasant duty to assist you in any manner you
may require.

G. W. C. T. It is a source of gratification
to us to find a Lodge ready for our services.
You will now give us, as representatives of the
Grand Lodge, a place with you, and we will
proceed with the installation ceremonies.

●

[*The W. C. T. and W. S. now step forward and conduct the officers to seats. The W. C. T. takes the G. W.
C. T., the W. S. the G. W. S., and the W. M. the G.
W. M. each to their respective stations. The W. C. T.
then steps in front of the G. W. C. T., who says*]

G. W. C. T. You have now closed your term
as Worthy Chief Templar of this Lodge. There
are certain laws which must be observed before
I am permitted to proceed, and in order to

know that you have complied with them, I will ask the usual questions :

G. W. C. T. Have the officers elect been chosen in accordance with the laws, and have the required bonds been given and approved?

W. C. T. They have.

G. W. C. T. Have the Quarterly Returns been made out, and, with the per centage, placed in the hands of the proper officer?

W. C. T. They have.

G. W. C. T. It is with pleasure that we receive your report, and, with the same feeling, I will proceed with the installation, as soon as the names of the appointed officers are reported to the Grand Worthy Secretary. The labors of your office are ended, yet your experience prepares you for still further usefulness, and the Lodge cannot now dispense with your services. You will therefore take your seat (*if re-elected, say " among the members,"*) as Past Worthy Chief Templar of this Lodge for the ensuing term.

[A full list of the officers elect, with blank spaces ready to fill in the names of the appointed officers, should be on the desk of the G. W. S., and, while the appointments are being made by the Officers elect, the G. W. M. will arrange seats in front of the G. W. C. T., as shown in the diagram:

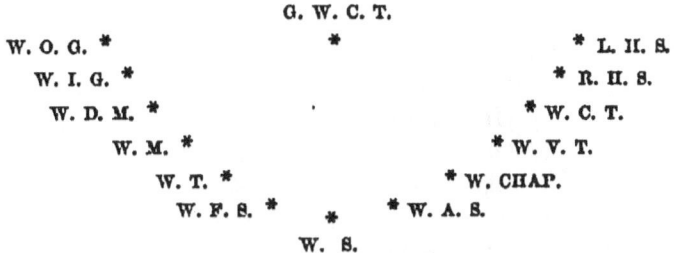

G. W. C. T.
*

W. O. G. *   * L. H. S.
　W. I. G. *   * R. H. S.
　　W. D. M. *   * W. C. T.
　　　W. M. *   * W. V. T.
　　　　W. T. *   * W. CHAP.
　　　　　W. F. S. *   *   * W. A. S.
　　　　　　W. S.

The regalia, except that of the Guards and Supporters, will be left at the chairs of the officers.]

G. W. C. T. (Rising.) My Brothers and Sisters, you have been elected to take charge of this Lodge for the ensuing quarter. It is no common mark of favor which has thus been bestowed upon you. I feel confident that it has been worthily bestowed, and that diligence in the discharge of all your duties, together with courteous demeanor, will raise you still higher in the estimation of your associates. In rising to the position of Officers of this Lodge, you have done well; but if you rise in the discharge of your duties, you will do better.

— Please sing our Installation Ode :

AIR—*"Auld Lang Syne."*

Whatever station we may fill
  In this exalted band,
Our plighted duties we shall still
  Achieve, with heart and hand ;
And evermore, through good and ill,
  By one another stand—
Whatever station we may fill
  In this exalted band.

G. W. C. T. The Officers will now assume the Good Templar attitude for receiving the

OBLIGATION.

You, and each of you, do solemnly promise, upon your sacred honor, that you will faithfully discharge all of the duties devolving upon you as Officers of this Lodge, in strict accordance with the laws, rules and usages of the Order, the Constitution and By-Laws of the Grand Lodge, and of this Lodge.

Officers respond. We will.

G. W. C. T. Brothers and Sisters, you have just heard the Obligation taken voluntarily by your Officers.

Members respond. We are witnesses.

●

\

[*Officers rise as they are addressed.*]

G. W. C. T. Worthy Guards, your duties require you to take charge of the doors of our Lodge : see to it that no unworthy persons are admitted, and that our Opening, Initiatory and Closing ceremonies are not disturbed. Our Grand Worthy Marshal will clothe you in regalia, and conduct you to your stations. You will relieve the present Guards, and immediately enter upon the discharge of your duties.

G. W. C. T. Worthy Marshal and Worthy Deputy Marshal, you will see that all who enter here without passing the Guards are qualified to remain; you will have charge of the Regalia and Odes, and will see that they are properly distributed at the opening and collected at the close of each meeting; conduct candidates at their initiation, and introduce visitors. Follow our Grand Worthy Marshal, and he will conduct you to your places in the Lodge, and clothe you with your regalia.

G. W. C. T. Worthy Financial Secretary and Worthy Treasurer, the financial affairs of this Lodge are now placed in your hands; see to it that no injustice or wrong is done to the Lodge or any of its members, or to yourselves. The Worthy Financial Secretary will, at the close of each meeting, pay all receipts to the Worthy Treasurer, and the Worthy Treasurer will keep the same subject to the order of the Lodge. You will now be conducted to your stations by our Grand Worthy Marshal, and enter upon the discharge of your duties. Let your fidelity be apparent, and a good conscience your reward.

G. W. C. T. Worthy Secretary and Worthy Assistant Secretary, the Records of this Lodge are now about to be placed in your keeping, and upon the precision, punctuality and ability of the Worthy Secretary, the prosperity and harmony of the Lodge in a great measure depend. A good Secretary is always at his post. Without prompt action on your part, the Worthy Chief Templar cannot successfully conduct the affairs of this Lodge. You have accepted an arduous place, but we feel confident that you have taken it with a determination to perform its duties faithfully. So do, and you will merit and receive the thanks of this Lodge and of the Grand Lodge. The Grand Worthy Marshal will now conduct you to your place, by the side of the Grand Worthy Secretary, and clothe you with regalia.

G. W. C. T. Worthy Chaplain, it is your privilege to invoke the divine favor and blessings, without which we labor in vain. Endeavor so to conduct the devotional exercises of this Lodge, that they may be beneficial to the members and acceptable to our Heavenly Father. The Grand Worthy Marshal will now conduct you to your place in the Lodge.

G. W. C. T. Worthy Vice Templar, you have, by the favor of your Brothers and Sisters, been placed in an important position. In the discharge of your duties, you are required to

assist in maintaining order, give out nightly a
retiring Pass-word, and superintend the Guards.
Be faithful, dignified, and prompt; and as you
discharge your duties, so will your merits be
appreciated by the Lodge. The Grand Worthy
Marshal will now conduct you to your place,
and clothe you in the regalia of your office.

G. W. C. T. Worthy Right and Left Hand
Supporters, your stations are indicated by the
names of your office. You will support your
Chief, and assist him as he shall from time to
time direct. (*They remain standing.*)

Worthy Chief Templar, you have been elected
to the highest office in the gift of this Lodge,
and you will consider it a mark of the esteem
and confidence the Lodge reposes in you. Let
it be your highest aim to merit a continuance
of their confidence, and to grow in their esteem.
Your duties are high and arduous. You are
the presiding and executive officer of this
Lodge, and you will see that order and the
rules of the Lodge are enforced, and that the
Lodge, in all of its workings, conforms to the
Ritual, the laws of the Right Worthy Grand

Lodge, your own Grand Lodge, and of this Lodge. It is expected that you will be in your place at every meeting, in time to commence at the regular hour; and upon the care and fidelity with which you discharge your duties, the welfare and prosperity of the Lodge principally depend. Be prompt, fearless and impartial in your acts; courteous and kind in your intercourse with the Lodge, and you will have the assistance of all the members in conducting its affairs, to your mutual profit and satisfaction.

Grand Worthy Marshal, you will now clothe the Supporters with regalia, and conduct them, with the Worthy Chief Templar, to their places.

Worthy Chief Templar, I now clothe you with the regalia of your office. Wear it with honor to yourself and profit to the Lodge. I also give to your keeping the Charter of the Lodge, which we all expect you will cherish and defend. I also present you a copy of the Constitution and By-Laws of this Lodge. These will guide you in conducting the ceremonies of our Order, and the admission of new members. And, lastly, I present you with the gavel: by this you will control the movements of the members, * * * will call to order, * * * will call up the members, * * * seats them again, and * * * will call up the officers. You will now enter upon the discharge of your duties.

● ● ●

G. W. C. T. Worthy Officers and Members, your Chief has been fully invested with his authority. I now wish to remind you that he alone cannot make this a successful, growing and profitable Lodge. He desires and expects your assistance in all that pertains to its welfare. Act together in harmony, in honor preferring one another; strive to excel in good words and works, remembering the object for which our noble Order was instituted, and its cardinal principles, as symbolized in our emblem and found in our motto—"Faith, Hope, and Charity." The Grand Lodge expects a good report from you, and the community that you will do a good work. I return you the thanks of the Grand Lodge and my own for the past, and as you are now in a condition to continue your noble work, may Heaven bestow upon you increased prosperity.

Please sing our Closing Installation Ode.

Air—"*The morning light is breaking.*"

Stand up, stand up for Temperance,
Ye soldiers of our cause;
Lift high our royal banner,
Nor let it suffer loss.
From victory to victory
Our army shall be led,
Till every foe is vanquished
And all are free indeed.

Stand up, stand up for Temperance,
Against unnumbered foes;
Your courage rise with danger,
And strength to strength oppose;
Forth to this mighty conflict—
Go, in this glorious hour—
Where duty calls, or danger,
Be never wanting there.

I now declare the officers of * * * Lodge, No. * * I. O. of G. T., duly installed, and authorized to enter upon and discharge their several duties for the term ending * * * 1st, 18 * * , and until their successors are elected and installed.

INSTITUTION.

The Officer instituting a new Lodge will satisfy himself, prior to the performance of his duties, that application has been made, in due form, for a Charter ; that the G. W. S. is in possession of the same, and that the fee has been paid.

On the night appointed for Institution, the G W. C. T, or his Deputy, shall take the Chair ; and, so far as may be in his power, shall appoint Members of the Order, in good standing, as acting Grand Officers. If, however, there are no Members of the Order present to assist him, he shall waive appointments pro tem., until after the applicants shall have been duly initiated.

The Grand Officer will then proceed with the Initiation Ceremony, as provided in the Ritual, with this difference only, that in cases where there are no members of the order present, as assistants, he will confer the Obligation of the Order, in due form, himself, and shall explain the several Charges of the Officers acting in connection with the Initiatory Work, so that the members of the newly instituted Lodge shall be enabled to proceed correctly in all future Initiations.

The applicants having been initiated, the Officer may proceed with the election and installation of the Officers, without conferring the Degrees ; but it shall be his duty to confer the Degrees within three months, so that after the first quarter the Officers, as far as required, shall be Degree members. He may, however, confer the Degrees the following evening.

After which the Grand Officer will examine the Charter of the Lodge, and see that it is duly filled out with the names of the members, name and number of the Lodge, location, date and proper signatures. He will then call up the Lodge, and proclaim as follows :

G. W. C. T. Brothers and Sisters : Having complied with all that our laws and usages demand, it is my pleasure and duty to welcome the members of ⁎ ⁎ ⁎ Lodge into union with our Temperance Fraternity. It is your prerogative, if you are but faithful and energetic, to exert a healthy influence upon the community in which you dwell;'to reform the inebriate, to assuage the woes and afflictions entailed upon our race by intemperance, and to suppress the traffic in alcoholic poisons, is one of the holiest of callings. Let your efforts ever be in harmony and unison, and your counsels together be tempered with reason, moderation, and the firmness of true wisdom. And, above all, let me ask that the example of this Lodge, and of the members thereof, shall ever be calculated to advance its true interests and those of our common cause. The perpetuity and salvation of an Institution or a Society depends more upon the example and practice of its members, than upon its mere precepts or its professions. Live above reproach; live to do good; live to improve all the higher and better faculties of man's nature; and, with the blessings of Providence, you will be instrumental in accomplishing a part of the great work of regenerating the world.

And now, by authority of the Grand Lodge of the Independent Order of Good Templars, I hereby declare * * * Lodge, No. * * * to be duly instituted and organized, and while obedient to the Constitution and decisions of the Grand Lodge, to be fully entitled to the rights and privileges of Lodges of our Order.

At the close of this Ceremony, any necessary business may be transacted, after which close the Lodge in form.

FUNERAL CEREMONY.

This Ceremony will be found in Chase's Digest, page 147.

www.ingramcontent.com/pod-product-compliance
Lightning Source LLC
Chambersburg PA
CBHW021237260626
47172CB00002B/808